A WALKING TOUR OF THE SHAMBLES

Little Walks for Sightseers, Number 16

NEIL GAIMAN & GENE WOLFE

ILLUSTRATED BY
RANDY BROECKER & EARL GEIER
FROM THEIR WORK IN
Ghost Stories of Old Street Illustrated

COVER BY GAHAN WILSON

By the same authors:

Neil Gaiman
Several Interesting Bus Journeys
Common Cucurbitae and how to identify them (Illustrated)
Little Walks for Sightseers Numbers 8, 11 and 24

Gene Wolfe
Thirteen Months in the Dessert
I Was a Werewolf for the C.I.A.
Handsaw: Escape from Wooden Cages
Six League Boots: Over the Alps in a Goat Cart
The Glass Key, or a Mysterious Florida Island
Handy Shambles Answer Book

A WALKING TOUR OF THE SHAMBLES

Little Walks for Sightseers, Number 16

The carving of "Captain" John Saunders discovered at Number One Old Street.

NEIL GAIMAN & GENE WOLFE

With illustrations by Randy Broecker and Earl Geier

Woodstock • 2009

A WALKING TOUR OF THE SHAMBLES
Little Walks for Sightseers, Number 16

Copyright © 2002 Neil Gaiman and Gene Wolfe.
Cover Artwork Copyright © 2002 Gahan Wilson.
Interior Artwork Pgs 2, 18, 38 Copyright © 2002 Earl Geier.
All other Interior Artwork Copyright © 2002 Randy Broecker.
All rights reserved.

Without limiting the rights under copyright reserved above, no part of this book may be reproduced in any form or by any electronic or mechanical means, including information storage and retrieval systems, without written permission from both the authors and publisher, except by a reviewer who may quote brief passages in review.

Dedication:
For R.A. Lafferty, who would have remembered all the tall tales he heard in Gavagan's.

Published by
American Fantasy Press
919 Tappan Street
Woodstock, Illinois, 60098

ISBN-10: 0-9610352-6-9
ISBN-13: 978-0-9610352-6-6

PRINTED IN THE UNITED STATES OF AMERICA

10 9 8 7 6 5 4 3

Third Printing, February 2009

Preface

Started as a public service in 1983 by a small local publisher loosely associated with the Chicago Tourist Commission, the Greater Chicago Chamber of Commerce and the International Brotherhood of Meatworkers, the *Little Walks for Sightseers* series has largely been credited with the economic and cultural revival of Chicago in the last two decades.

One volume, however, has been the subject of controversy and speculation since its first (and only) publication several years ago. (The exact date of publication is still hotly disputed by collectors.)

We bring this book back into print now only as a service to collectors of the *Little Walks For Sightseers* series. There are, after all, many good reasons why the initial printing was removed from bookstores, libraries, and, where necessary, bedrooms, by law enforcement agencies and employees of the Chicago Tourist Commission.

Firstly, the area described herein does not exist.

Secondly, should the area described herein actually exist, any journeys, expeditions, or visitations to, from, or in the Shambles would be strongly and actively discouraged by the Greater

Chicago Chamber of Commerce and the Chicago Tourist Commission.

Thirdly, both Gene Wolfe and Neil Gaiman, eminent authors, respected men in their fields, with wives, extensive families, and a lot to lose should the International Brotherhood of Meatworkers take a more active interest in the case, now both deny having written any part of this book.

Fourthly, there are a number of easily proven falsehoods in here: H.H. Holmes' House of Horrors was in Englewood, Illinois, not in this illusory "Shambles", and the good Doctor was brought to justice in 1895, not 1884. There could not have been two such houses, two such men, two such acid baths: the gods themselves would forbid it.

Fifthly, nobody has been paid off. Nobody has disappeared. There is no website at www.preserveusfromthehouseofclocks.com, no blood on the skirting board, no significance to how deeply the parsley has sunk into the butter.

We trust this clears the matter up once and for all,

The Publishers.

A WALKING TOUR OF THE SHAMBLES
Little Walks for Sightseers, Number 16

"There was a little feller,
and they found him in the celler,
and his skin was going yeller
and his eyes had gone away . . ."

— Popular children's song
Shambles circa 1945

NEIL GAIMAN & GENE WOLFE

With illustrations from Ghost Stories of Old Street Illustrated

OLD STREET

DESTINATIONS OF NOTE:
Number One • Number Two • Number Two-A • Number Two-and-a-Half B • Chinese-American Burial Temple • American Chestnut • Number Three: Blind House • Number Eight: Shambles Shop • Number Nine: Cereal House • Number Seven

Neil Gaiman and Gene Wolfe

While this walking tour will cover a distance of only three city blocks, the compilers of this guide book suggest, based on our experience, that tourists and the curious be prepared to devote an entire day to it; there will be much to see and experience in your walk.

Our walking tour begins in Old Street.

Walking past **Number One Old Street**, pause to observe the fine carving over the front door. Believed for many years to be a gargoyle, this carving was discovered, during a cleaning in 1983, to be that of "Captain" John Saunders, a prominent inhabitant of the area in the 1880s. Strangely, however, there is no record of Saunders ever having lived in this house. The roof was restored following the Chicago Fire. (Fortunately for the amateur historian and the lover of fine architecture, the whole of the area commonly known as the Shambles was almost completely untouched by the Fire.)

Number One Old Street was built in 1883 as the home of Harold Brennan, an eminent citizen of the time. Brennan, a banker, was also well-known as the founder of the Organization for the Humane Treatment of Cab-Horses. He was arrested in 1907 for sending poison pen letters (described by the then commissioner of police as "unusually vile") to visiting opera singers and clergymen. The handwriting was unquestionably identified as Brennan's by several of his clerks. Harold Brennan committed suicide in a holding cell while awaiting trial, hanging himself with his

A Walking Tour of The Shambles

leather belt. The poison pen letters, however, continued unabated, the last one received in 1912 by Miss Flora Lovat, who was appearing in *Iolanthe*, in the title role, at the Gaiety Opera.

In private hands until the Second World War, the house was bought in 1953 by the Summer Corporation, a multinational corporation with extensive interests.

Strolling across the street, we find ourselves at **Number Two-A Old Street**. This house is, as you will see immediately, remarkable for a number of reasons. The building itself is no more than 12 feet wide, and the front door is less than four feet high. The house has been described as an architectural novelty, and was originally built by Nathan Huckle, the original builder of #2 Old Street, next door, as a playhouse for his children.

Following the death of both children and Mrs. Huckle in a tragic boating accident, the house was closed up. It was purchased in 1931 by "Colonel" Lucius Little and his wife, Myrna, as a holiday house between their professional engagements.

The present owners purchased the house from the Colonel's grandchildren (who were both of normal height). The Board of Tourism would like to remind sightseers not to knock on the door of #2A, nor to disturb the present owners in any way. If by any chance you do encounter the owner or her sons, do not accept food from them.

Number Two, Old Street. *"One of the finest private houses in the whole of the environs of the Windy City."* So wrote the Home and Hearth Correspondent of *Fireside* magazine, in May 1911. *"Not wholly because of the high ceilings, the Viennese Woodwork, or the Venetian Glass windows, but because, as this reporter can asseverate without fear of contradiction, the flower gardens—the 'bowers of delight' as Mrs. Parrish put it so perfectly—are the most beautiful in the entire state of Illinois. The Rose Walk has no competition in the city, save for the Grape Arbor, and the fountain display can have no equal for beauty, unless it be the Japanese Pond."*

While the House (since 1970 the Headquarters of the International Brotherhood of Meatworkers) has remained in excellent condition (guided tours of all the floors except, of course, the fifth, by arrangement, Tuesdays and Thursdays, at 11:00 am sharp), the ornamental gardens, the pagoda, the arbors and carp ponds have long since become the site of a multistory parking lot.

This lot (**Number Two-and-a-Half B**) is one of the Shambles' taller buildings, and is open to

A Walking Tour of The Shambles

you, being wholly automated. Enter on Old Street or Abattoir Alley. Take a ticket from the conveniently located machine, and the arm will lift. Do not attempt to take the watch from the wrist of the arm. The roof may be reached by strolling past the seventeenth level along the interior spiral. (No skateboarding.) Or by use of the escaladder marked Varlets Only. (Number Two and-a-Half B provides Varlet Parking for the Lake Shoridan on Lake Shore Drive.) Visitors attracted to the convenience of the escaladder may wish to de-rung immediately should the direction of climb become reversed, as sometimes happens. (See below.)

Lake Michigan will be in easy view, east, from the roof. The Rent-a-Rifle kiosk is open Tuesday through Sunday, in good weather only. Costs vary with caliber and shots fired. (Six for the price of five, most calibers.) We think a telescopic sight well worth the added fee. Note that the rifles are *for lake use only* both sail and powered craft.

To the north, you will observe the proud black spire of the Sears Tower, Chicago's highest building. Its observation deck can be viewed from this point in the Shambles. (The Shambles itself, however, cannot be seen from the observation deck of the Sears Tower; this is because the observation deck overlooks the Shambles.) The one-hundred-ten story Tower contains seventy-six thousand tons of steel and enough concrete to build a six-lane highway to Mars. It is thought to be the only U.S. skyscraper to have bullet-proof windows more than thirteen hundred feet above street level.

Southward notice the Old Main Post Office, the glory of Depression Era Chicago, erected across the Eisenhower Expressway by President Roosevelt. Although a focus of civic pride for many years, its constant collisions with trucks and cars posed a perpetual problem that the U.S. Postal Service was never able to resolve in a satisfactory manner. It is no longer in use, but serves as a storage facility for undelivered mail.

To the west rises the windowless wall of a large grey building we have been unable to identify.

If you boldly remain on the escaladder as it descends past ground level, you will be carried past twelve levels of subterranean parking. The escaladder terminates on the level below the twelfth, which you may view by flashlight (if you are so provided) or by striking matches. The Light Switch is on the wall to your left at a distance of about four hundred feet. (Or eighty paces.) *Do not touch it.* Directly ahead of you, beyond the reservoir of blind fish, you will see the entrance to the tunnel leading to the caverns below Lake Michigan. (Fully described in *Little Walking Tours, Number 22*). To your right is the **Chinese-American Burial Temple**, the tallest

A Walking Tour of The Shambles

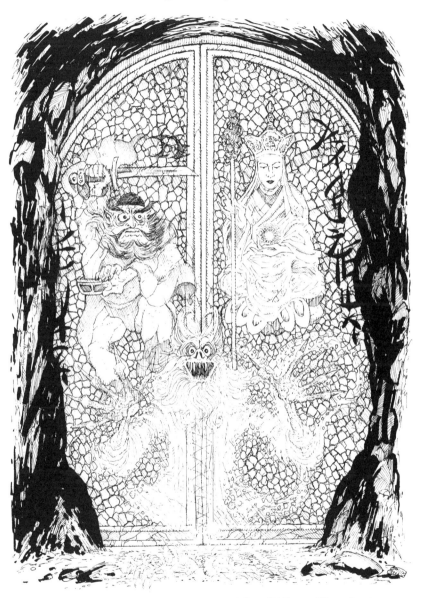

The stunning portraits of Zhong Kui and Ti-Tsang Wang dazzle visitors from around the worlds.

underground structure in the city. Constructed in 1871 to house the remains of Chinese who were refused burial in California (then the site of much anti-Chinese violence), its subterranean location and other safeguards have protected it from the relentless destruction of ethnic neighborhoods. The key beneath the mat is for the convenience of Chinese-American funeral directors. Do not use it, or enter the Chinese-American Burial Temple by other means. For informational purposes only, you should be aware the Chinese ghosts are compounded of human and animal characteristics. Should you meet another sightseer having either a tail, hairy ears, or both, be polite but do not accompany him (or her) to any suggested destination unless he (or she) displays a copy of this guide book and permits you to open it. In general, distrust anyone you may meet whose teeth are sharper than your own. This is good advice throughout Chicago and applies with particular force to members or supposed members of the International Brotherhood of Meatworkers.

To your left, beyond the Light Switch and the Grape Arbor, is one of the area's least known but most interesting attractions, the stump of a large **American Chestnut** in which the Chicago Fire still smolders. The superstitious believe that this fire will break out again when the city is visited

A Walking Tour of The Shambles

by a descendant of Molly O'Leary. Beyond the Fiery Stump lies the entrance to Plicate Lane, leading to Lower Wacker Drive. Note that Plicate Lane leads out of the Shambles; it is not possible to return to the Shambles via Plicate Lane or Lower Wacker. Use the escaladder to return to the surface, should you wish to do so. You may exit the parking lot either by paying the ticket you took upon entering or by ducking under the arm blocking the exit. Should you choose the latter means of egress, run.

American Chestnut roasted by an open fire.

Neil Gaiman and Gene Wolfe

Returning to Old Street, **Number Three** (of stone painted white) is the famous **Blind House** built by Eden Flamm in eighteen seventy-two. Being totally blind, he resolved to construct it without windows in order to conserve heat. His neighbors objected, and his compromise is the structure you observe, whose "windows" do not in fact communicate with the interior and admit neither light nor air. Flamm employed only blind servants, but had difficulty keeping them, as they declared the house haunted and complained that they were clutched by unseen hands as they went about their duties. The "ghost" was eventually discovered to be a young man named Muadh Kelly who, having read de Maupasant's "The Horla," had resolved to become invisible. He is believed to have been killed by Flamm, who toward the latter part of his life went armed with two revolvers and fired at any slight unexpected sound. The interior may not be seen. The real estate broker's sign in the window to your left is spurious, belonging to an agency long defunct. Note the telephone number provided, consisted of two letters and five numerals. (Such numbers are no longer in use.) You are advised not to call this number.

☞☜

Number Eight, next to Number Two, now houses an interesting store in which this guidebook and many other useful and curious items

A Walking Tour of The Shambles

may be obtained. (Notice that this book is in the shop, which itself is in this book—an infinite progression.) The **Shambles Shop** is perhaps most famous for its assortment of wax fruit, of one hundred and forty-seven kinds and degrees of ripeness. These are the particular pride of Ms. Cherry Bly, one of the owners. Called "Fruit Fly" in high school when her science class performed experiments in genetics, she had turned this derogatory nickname against its originators by developing and marketing astonishingly lifelike wax fruit flies created by dipping living fruit flies into very hot coloured waxes. A well known geneticist at the University of Chicago is said to have been duped more than once by wax flies obtained from the Shambles Shop by prankish students.

Ghost Stories of Old Street Illustrated, the self-published production of a well known resident of the district, is another popular Shambles Shop item. A copy will provide the curious with much interesting lore beyond the provenance of the present guide. It is alleged, for example, that "Horla" Kelly continues to haunt Number Three, and many terrifying tales in the book detail his exploits, though without basis in fact beyond the failure of the police to find his body in the dark. Similarly, "Captain" Saunders is said to have laid a curse upon anyone staring at his likeness (above the door of Number One, above) for longer than one quarter of one minute. Such persons, it is said, will never return to the Shambles once they have left it, and will be unable even to find it again. Another legend relates that no one who has not studied "Captain" Saunders' features can obtain a commercial driver's license at any facility in Cook County without offering a ruinously large bribe. While no thinking person takes such legends seriously, it is true that it is close to impossible to get a taxi in the Shambles area, while bus service is nonexistent.

To return from fantasy to reality, the Shambles Shop also carries organic produce and herbal preparations, as well as one-size-fits all clothing and study aids.

Number Nine, across Old Street, is called **Cereal House**. Its name is, of course, a reference to the sculptured sheaves of wheat, oats, and rye that so tastefully embellish its capitals and cornices. This graceful Greek Revival home was completed in 1868, work having been suspended for a time due to the U.S. Civil War. Charming and luxurious, yet cozy, it is owned by the Collins Family and operated as a bed-and-breakfast by Robert and Willa Stevenson (nee Collins). There are seven bedrooms, of which two have private baths. All are large, and all are tastefully furnished with antiques. Prices range from seventy dollars to one hundred and twenty-five, the price for the Black Room, which

A Walking Tour of The Shambles

boasts (in addition to its own bathroom with sauna) the original Terribly Strange Bed, an heirloom of Willa's family. Guests are asked to provide names and telephone numbers of next of kin, which adds to the atmosphere. Be sure to do this. Room prices include the famous Seven Cereal Breakfast, seven small bowls containing seven superb breakfast cereals seldom if ever seen in the United States. "A Lodging for the Night" is the motto of the Cereal House, but it actually offers the weary tourist much, much more.

Between Number Nine Old Street and its neighbour is an alleyway leading to Saunders Park. In *Ghost Stories of Old Street Illustrated* we are informed that only small children and the dead use this alley with impunity; however, in this we can detect a touch of local leg-pulling: your authors have observed, on several occasions, a stenographer, and on one occasion an official from the Brotherhood of Meatworkers, using this alley as a short-cut.

Passing this alley as quickly as possible we come to **Number Seven, Old Street**. There is nothing interesting in any way about Number Seven. Built in the mid 1970s, it is architecturally and socially devoid of significance. There are maps of the area which do not show Number Seven on them, but these maps are out

Neil Gaiman and Gene Wolfe

The Short Cut.

of date, or were drawn by unreliable cartographers.

An amusing legend, told to one of your authors by several of the locals in Gavagan's Irish Saloon, has Number Seven appearing, fully built, on a corner that was once an empty lot, following a particularly vivid meteor shower in 1974, and adds that several would-be housebreakers have attempted to gain entry, and have either never been seen again, or have reappeared working on a shrimp boat in Galveston, Texas owned by a religious brotherhood known as the Sons of the Moon.

Note the remarkable mushroom crop on the grass, and on the boles and trunks of the trees. (Best seen at dusk when their colours are at their most vivid, and their natural luminescence is most visible.) The owners of the house have asked us to mention here that these fungi are, in the main, not for human consumption, and that, in extreme circumstances, it can be quite the reverse.

MEAT STREET

DESTINATIONS OF NOTE:
Number Twelve: House of Clocks •
Saunders Park (including: the Petting Zoo, Ornamental Lake, Haunted House, Bakingham Fountain, the Botanical Forest, Swan Boat Dock, Statue of Captain Saunders, The Maze, The Dutch Garden, & The Garden for the Blind)
• **Holmes House** • **First Church of The Sailor Return'd**

Neil Gaiman and Gene Wolfe

Here we come to the intersection of Old Street and Meat Street.

We shall turn left down Meat Street. (Turning right will take us from the Shambles to, on weekdays, North Shore Drive. On weekends the street is closed completely. On several Feast Days, High Holy Days, and on Presidents' Day, unsuspecting visitors who take a right turn may often find themselves in Waukegan.)

☞

Number Twelve, Meat Street, our next destination, can, on the hour and the quarter-hour, be heard from several blocks away, for this is, as seen on national television, the **House of Clocks**.

The House of Clocks opens at 9:00 am, seven days a week, and closes at 6:00 pm sharp. Tickets can be bought in the gatehouse, in the Shambles Shop in Old Street, or purchased with a credit card over the internet *(www.preserveusfromthehouseofclocks.com)*. Pause before entering to look up at the clock tower: a dome surmounted by a small teapot. At 9.00 am, midday, 3.00 pm and 6.00 pm, a mechanical figure will travel slowly from the door on the left to the door on the right, pausing mid-way to strike the bell with a small hammer or gavel it holds. According to the official guide-book this figure represents former president Warren Gamaliel Harding, although even through a binoculars the

A Walking Tour of The Shambles

face cannot be made out clearly enough for any definite identification.

The Harding Bell is just one of at least 20,000 clocks in the House of Clocks, collected, discovered and accumulated by the former owner, Margaux Brown, between 1915 and her death in 1969. Despite approaches from Ripley's Believe It Or Not, and from the Walt Disney Corporation, the House of Clocks has remained in private hands, and is maintained as it was in Margaux Brown's day.

The House of Clocks employs several dozen keepers, each a horological specialist, to maintain, repair, observe and guard the timepieces in their care, and to ensure that the stairways are kept open.

On the ground floor you may see a number of pocket-watches, hunters, repeaters, and several unique wrist-watches.

The second floor is devoted to grandfather clocks, grandmother clocks, and to the only American display of great-grandfather clocks. Do not be alarmed by these strange-looking timepieces: remember, they cannot climb stairs.

The highlight of the collection on the third floor is the L'Horloge D'Or of Marie Antoinette, bought by Margaux Brown at auction in 1951. This gold-encrusted, mirrored timepiece is justly famed in horological circles, both for its gilded beauty and for its tendency to temporal reflectivity and transmutation. Several times the authors of this guide have set off to see it, getting up early and packing sandwiches, and have spent many happy hours walking down the fifty feet of corridor leading to L'Horloge D'Or, only frustrated in their quest by the announcement from one of the keepers of the clocks that closing time was fast approaching.

The fourth floor contains surrealist timepieces, ranging from the Cartier Dali Soft Watches, to the Cheese Clocks, the Water Clocks (salt and freshwater), and, in its own refrigerated display case, the Ice Clock. The Meat Clock, a donation in 1967 from the International Brotherhood of Meatworkers, is no longer on public display, although the soft and melodious hum of the flies it attracts is omnipresent, and some claim that it may be heard howling, like a wolf, on the hour and half-hour.

The clocks on the fifth floor, although at first glance less impressive than those you will have seen so far, attain significance upon reading the labels. These were the clocks of various famed and celebrated personages of yesteryear. Listen to the gentle tick-tock-tick of William Ewart Gladstone's alarm clock; to the ribald tock tock-tock of James Thurber's travel clock; the tut-tut-tutting of the Imperial Timepiece of Joshua Norton; and the swish-swish of the clock that Douglas Fairbanks presented to Mary Pickford on the occasion of their engagement. From the balcony on the north wing of the fifth floor there is a fine view of Saunders Park, although to reach it one must walk though the Rogue's

A Walking Tour of The Shambles

Gallery of clocks, including a clock that belonged to either Burke or Hare, the mantel-clock Elizabeth Borden inherited from her papa, the clocks of Albert Fish, Edward Gein, and of Renwick Williams (the original "West End Monster"). All of these clocks remain, for obvious reasons, unwound and silent.

Taking the backstairs down through the House of Clocks, the gift shop, on the ground floor, will be your final stop.

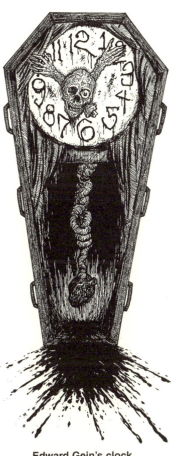

Edward Gein's clock.

Here postcards, novelties (chronistic and anachronistic), candy timepieces, and reproduction clocks and watches can be purchased. A popular decorative novelty is the "Hours of Your Life" chart which describes, with precision, how many hours you have to live, and the method and time of your death. The Charts are suitable for framing, although for an additional $30 they can be purchased already-framed.

Pay special attention to the sundials that line the walk as you leave; know that they will be paying special attention to you.

Returning to the sidewalk, the sightseer is now faced with a choice: to return to Meat Street, or to enter Saunders Park.

Saunders Park provides an oasis of calm and silence after the bustle of the streets. Listen carefully. Can you hear the ticking of the great-grandfather clocks in the House of Clocks? If so, is it becoming louder? The crocodile ticks too; you should have no difficulty distinguishing its rapid *tick-tick-tick* from the weighty *TICK* and *TOCK* of the great-grandfather clocks. Take warning from this—the crocodile can move fast as well.

Should you distinguish the characteristic tinny note of the crocodile, proceed briskly to the shore of the **Ornamental Lake.** Follow the path *counterclockwise* around the lake. The crocodile will try to gain a march on you by swimming directly across the lake to the **Swan Boat Dock.** (It will leave a clearly visible wake upon the surface of the water, unless there is a wind. Note, however, that it may be as far as eight feet in advance of that wake.) At the Dock, your best stratagem is to board a Swan Boat,

A Walking Tour of The Shambles

provided that one is available. Shut the gate (above the swan's tail) at once. The Swan Boats have high sides and sturdy gates (except nos. 6, 9, and 13) formidable barriers to the crocodile. Furthermore, your Swandolier will discourage it with his sculling oar. You are expected to tip for this service.

Your ride about the Ornamental Lake should be peaceful and pleasant. It will, moreover, provide a welcome opportunity to sit down for a half hour or so. This will also be a good time to consult the "Hours of Your Life" chart, provided you have purchased one. Note that the times quoted are Greenwich Mean Time. You will have to correct for Central Standard Time and Daylight Savings Time. When it is Tea Time in Greenwich, it is Breakfast Time in Chicago, and so on. (It is always Tea Time in Wonderland. See below.) Should "method of demise" be listed as "crocodile," *"Crocodylus toculionis barrie."* or "horological" you should be cautious throughout the remainder of your tour. If you discover this on Christmas Eve, Yom Kippur, or President's Day, you are well advised to leave the Swan Boat and run—rather quickly—to Old Street via Meat Street. Proceed straight through the intersection, to get to the relative safety of Waukegan, (the birthplace of the famous comedian Jack Benny and the site of Jack Benny School and the subject of *Little Walks for Sightseers, Number 39.*) We caution you to remember the swiftness of the crocodile.

Neil Gaiman and Gene Wolfe

If you decide to continue your Swan Boat ride, we salute you. At the west end of the Ornamental Lake, you will be treated to a unique view of the statue of "Captain Saunders", (described below). The woman crouching at his feet is Washington Socialite Rose Greenhow O'Neil. The lovely Widow O'Neil, as she was known to her many admirers, drowned in 1864 when she leaped into the sea from the deck of the blockade-runner *Condor* (J.S. Saunders commander) following a trip to England.

Proceeding around the Ornamental Lake, observe the entrance to the Saunders Park Petting Zoo. This highly imaginative gateway takes the form of the open mouth of a python, the famed Saunders Park Python having long been one of the chief attractions of the Petting Zoo. (See below.) The gateway was financed through the untiring efforts of the Ladies of the International Sisterhood of Meat Workers and is maintained by their male counterparts, who may often be observed repainting it and cleaning the teeth with files.

Beyond the Petting Zoo, the Greensward gives a clear view of West Old Street, and the magnificent Victorian Holmes House. (called the House of Horrors by the yellow journalists of its time. See below.) When Mr. H.H. Holmes was in residence, the third floor was occupied by his children. Thus the elaborate cast-iron bars.

Flanking the Greensward opposite the Petting Zoo is the Haunted House operated by

A Walking Tour of The Shambles

the Meatworkers from the first Friday in October through Halloween. You will note that it is a two-thirds scale model of Holmes House.

Next viewed is the Maze, said to be a replica of the famed Covent Garden Maze in England. This cannot be correct, as there is no Covent Garden Maze in England. Coven Garden may be intended.

Beyond the Maze, the swan-borne sightseer may observe the Dutch Garden, with the Gazing Ball at its center. The Gazing Ball may be safely viewed at this distance, although not by pregnant women. Passing the gay (and straight) tulip beds of the Dutch Garden, your eye will surely be drawn to the **Bakingham Fountain**, given to Saunders Park by the Summer Corporation, well-known for its molasses-and mayonnaise glazed hams as well as its nonpareil Summer Mayonnaise Potato Salad. (This was the salad famously misspelled by Vice President Dan Quayle, who had sampled some.) The beautiful trees bordering the lawn about the Bakingham Fountain represent the extreme westward (or possibly southern) margin of the Botanical Forest.

This now brings you around to your point of entry to Saunders Park, **the Botanical Forest**, which you passed rapidly upon leaving the Sun Dial Garden of the House of Clocks. From the relative safety of the boat, you will now have time and leisure to observe the many rare and interesting specimens it contains. At this point

Neil Gaiman and Gene Wolfe

The Petting Zoo is a favorite with children.

in your voyage, your Swandolier may sing, or request permission to sing. Grant it. It is in both your interests.

Back at the Swan Boat Dock, pay and tip your Swandolier and congratulate him upon his baritone (tenor, bass, soprano). Do not make jokes turning on the "swan song" supposedly sung at death. He will pretend not to understand.

Resuming the path that carried you to the Swan Boat Dock proceed counterclockwise around the lake. Pause at the **Statue of "Captain" Saunders**. Do not over-look the face. The soldiers in Confederate uniform depicted on the base are members of Henry H. Young's Union Army command, dressed and equipped to deceive the foe. The men dressed as Union

A Walking Tour of The Shambles

Dragoons are in fact members of Eighth Texas Cavalry, which adopted the blue uniform of the enemy for the same reason. "Captain" Saunders served in both units, often at the same time. The enchanting flower beds around the base of the statue are maintained in all their beauty by the Daughters of Tara. It is unwise to step into, or disparage, them.

Should you be accompanied by children, you will want to visit the **Saunders Park Petting Zoo**, particularly if the children accompanying you are not your own. The Petting Zoo's collection of friendly farm animals includes (but is not limited to) chickens, turkeys, ducks, geese, rabbits, guinea pigs, Poland China pigs (with piglets), goats of three different breeds, kids, lambs, rams, ewes, donkeys, wolves, mice, rats, cats, dogs, dodos, eaglets, calves, cows, a longhorn steer, a Jersey bull, colts, mares, geldings, stallions, griffins, turtles (both legitimate and mock), a lory, owls, monkeys, fish, and frogs, all of which the children are permitted and in fact encouraged to pick up and handle. At the Big Red Barn they may watch a cow being milked or a foal being gelded. There is also an eel pond; Old Bill, the attendant, can frequently be prevailed upon to balance an eel on the end of his nose to entertain the little ones.

We were lucky enough to make the acquaintance of the carpenter (then repairing the fifty-foot wooden tank provided for the walrus). He has become great friends with his charge, and entertained us by detailing their adventures. You are cautioned, however, to discourage children who may be inclined to follow the white rabbit into his burrow.

The pythoness will permit well-behaved children to stroke her reptile companion, the Saunders Park Python, and will tell your fortune, or the children's, for a small fee. Some children we saw were privileged to hear these prognostications while romping with the python, and received them with rapt attention.

Continuing along the path around the lake, you see the Greensward, a sweeping expanse of well-tended lawn available for croquet, pick-up football games, and the training and exercising of dogs. There are no "keep off the grass" signs here! But watch your step.

Unless you have chosen to make an October visit, the **Haunted House** will be closed. The screams heard to issue from it upon several occasions are related to wiring problems that trigger its sound effects at odd hours. You should be aware that it is a felony to remove, tamper with, or cross the police crime-scene tape.

The Maze is one of the proudest and most interesting features of Saunders Park. Its walls are comprised of barberry, holly, hawthorn, concrete, and barbed wire. Its multifold turnings are said to confuse even members of the International Brotherhood of Meatworkers, several of whom will be found wandering its

A Walking Tour of The Shambles

convoluted corridors on any fine night. The tunnel at its center provides rapid egress to Lower Wacker Drive and the caverns beneath Lake Michigan. It is large, well ventilated, and well lit, at least in its earlier reaches.

The Dutch Garden beyond is itself a species of maze. A single but convoluted path leads the visitor through low beds of beautiful flowers to the Gazing Ball at its center. Beyond the Gazing Ball lies the **Garden for the Blind**.

Again we return to the arbors of the Botanical Forest and where you entered Saunders Park. It is unwise to return to the House of Clocks via the path by which you left it. This was pointed out to us, beautifully yet forcefully, by a small child we encountered in the Petting Zoo. "How doth the little crocodile," she lisped, "improve his shining tail, and pour the waters of the Nile, on every golden scale. How cheerfully he seems to grin . . ." There was more, but she had made her point.

As we walk north on Meat Street the happy sounds of Saunders Park echo into nothing so quickly that we might believe our whole stay there to have been nothing more than a dream by a river, on a summer's day.

On the south side of the road we pass a wall, built of local stone, which the locals are given to using as an art gallery, a message board, and an impromptu meeting place. It was beside this wall that H.H. Holmes was finally apprehended by Daniel Murphy, the celebrated Pinkerton detective, who was the only one to see through his disguise as a gin-soaked beggarwoman. (*"They looked at the face,"* wrote Murphy, in his celebrated monograph on the subject. *"I, on the other hand, looked at the fingers, hairy-knuckled with dark blood crusted beneath the well manicured fingernails, and I knew I had found my man."*) A painting of the historic capture may be seen in the front room of the Cereal House on Old Street, above the fireplace.

A public subscription was taken up at the time, to raze the **Holmes House** to the ground; however following representations from two women, neither of whom are believed to have been married to Mr. Holmes, and who, for all practical purposes, denied ever having met him, but who were able to demonstrate that they were indeed the joint-owners of the mortgage to the ill-fated house, the building was simply moved in its entirety several blocks to its current location on West Old Street, while the infamous cellar was filled in with rubble and fragments of brick, and paved over. Its exact original location is no longer known. (The plaque outside 13 Canal Street is a hoax, put up in 1976 by the customers at Gavagan's Irish Saloon, immediately across the street.)

Walk on. You might wish to know that the iron hand-pump set in the sidewalk to your

A Walking Tour of The Shambles

right was padlocked by order of the Mayor of Chicago, following the cholera outbreak of 1866, and remains so to this day. Many locals stroke or pat it for luck as they pass. The practice among local children of playing the dare-game of "lick the drip" has long since been eliminated; please do nothing to encourage its return—refreshments, including water, beer, juices and soft drinks, may be purchased at Molly Graw's Restaurant in Canal Street, and at the Shambles Shop in Old Street.

Crossing the road we encounter the **First Church of The Sailor Return'd**. Built in 1870, and rebuilt, following local disturbances, in 1894 and 1933, this Church was endowed and erected by "Captain" John Saunders, following his triumphant return from distant shores (most local histories claim that these were on the South China Sea, but there is much circumstantial evidence to the contrary). The design is unusual for a place of worship. The carvings on the West Wall, which is all that remains of the original 1870 church building, are at the time of writing, once again on public display, following a lengthy period of time hidden under blank canvas, and are believed to represent the apocalypse, or possibly a Stygian fish-market.

When not in use for services, the church is

commonly locked. The key, however, may be readily obtained from the verger, who lives in the small grey house next door (the house is unnumbered, presumably for religious reasons, but is unmistakable). If there is no answer to the door-bell, the spare key to the main door of the church is to be found under the door mat, or beneath the pot of geraniums on the left of the front door. Leave the verger a note to say that you have it.

Entering the church, the sightseer is struck by the smell: a fresh, salty smell, with overtones of iodine and gentle hints of rotting kelp. Do not light any of the candles you may see. The smell will only get worse. Also, the candles are, according to the verger, only to be used ceremonially. Do not worry about the lack of windows. Your eyes will adjust to the dimness soon enough, and many of the objects and hangings in the church, being of nautical origin, have their own phosphorescence, which will help.

The congregation of the Church was swelled by over 800 in 1915, following the unfortunate sinking of the top-heavy S.S. Eastland before it left the shore, and although congregants are no longer as numerous as once they were, sailors, fisherman and holidaymakers still venture unwisely onto Lake Michigan, and come to the Shambles to celebrate their return to dry land.

The stone floor can be slippery. Watch your step as you go.

The church may well have been designed by

A Walking Tour of The Shambles

"Captain" John Saunders himself, and his unfamiliarity with liturgical tradition would account for many of its peculiarities: the centrally-placed altar, for example, covered with the skin of what seems to be a flayed sea-beast, and covered with a profusion of enormous cowries, conches and cones, may be a representation of the altar that Saunders might have encountered on his travels; while the open pit, or well, that leads down from the western transept is thought to have been used as a graphic representation to the congregation of the fall from grace. There is a crypt, although there are not, as was claimed in a 1931 newspaper article, catacombs.

Keep your back to the wall, where possible.

In the niche above the door, visible only during a service when all candles are lit, or by flashlight beam, is a statue thought to have been brought back from distant shores, possibly by "Captain" John Saunders. It is striking, both in its multiplicity of ivory limbs, and in its single eye—erroneously claimed to be the largest cabochon-cut emerald in the world (in fact the Klimpt Emerald, currently on display in the Royal Museum in Stockholm, is believed to be at least one quarter of a carat heavier). The torso is exquisite gold filigree on pink coral, while the tiny, half-devoured elephants that hang at its side are carved from one single block of white jade. While possessing no obvious religious significance, it is a striking piece of

Neil Gaiman and Gene Wolfe

This idol keeps a watchful eye on the Church from its dark niche.

primitive art, and is of enormous cultural value.

Several times in the last century the emerald has been stolen, followed on each occasion by the disappearance (presumably also by theft) of the statue itself. On each occasion the statue has been returned anonymously: intact, polished, restored and, according to the verger, with an expression of satisfaction on its face. (*If*, the verger, a stickler for detail, adds, *that is its face, of course.*)

The white-painted door at the back of the chancel leads to the walled graveyard at the rear of the church. An oddly cheerless place, one can only hope that the collection for the restoration fund reaches its goal sooner rather

A Walking Tour of The Shambles

than later, and that the graves and the crypts can be returned to the condition in which their inhabitants would have wished to have been interred in them. Until this time, historians and sightseers are not advised to walk through the graveyard alone. The foolhardy, or the dedicated scholar, may obtain maps to the graveyard, stout sticks and cudgels, and small meat cakes from the verger, in exchange for a small donation to the graveyard restoration fund.

Once you are outside the church, look up: the carved gutter-spouts are particularly deserving of attention. Thought for many years to be carvings in caricature of many of the local luminaries whose burial places may be found in the graveyard, including Harold Brennan, Nathan Huckle, Eden Flamm, Procrustes Collins, and Rose Greenhow O'Neil, they were discovered in the 1970s simply to be reproductions in cheap marble of several of the gargoyles of Notre Dame de Paris, bought by the then chaplain as a job lot from a builders' yard in Sheboygan in 1932.

Do not forget to return the church key to the verger, nor to return to him any items you might, absent-mindedly have picked up during your walk around the interior of the church. Virtue is its own reward. No questions will be asked, nor will you be laughed at.

Turning left as you exit will bring you to Canal Street.

CANAL STREET

**DESTINATIONS OF NOTE:
Molly Graw's Restaurant • Hair Today • Vorm Apartments • Gavagan's Irish Saloon**

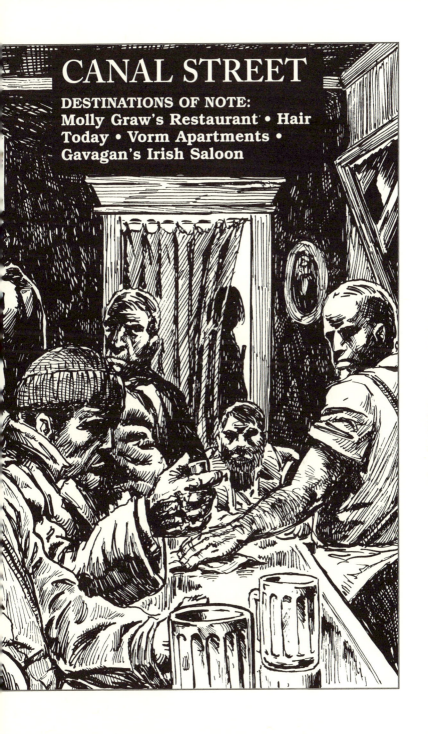

Neil Gaiman and Gene Wolfe

Since Canal Street[1] was filled in, in 1921, we have only old photographs of the street as it once was to remind us of the past, when Canal Street really did border a canal, originally intended to lead from Lake Michigan directly to Hannibal, Missouri, linking Chicago directly with the Mississippi. The Canal Company claimed that water would be a cheaper and easier method of transportation than the then-ubiquitous railroads, but the world was never to find out if this were true or not. Funding ran out at the end of Canal Street, and now all that remains of the Hannibal Canal is the boating pond in Saunders Park. (Those who claim that the Swandoliers and their swandolas have been trapped there since both ends of the Canal were closed and filled in, in 1921, are, in fact, romanticizing. The Swandoliers are free to leave the park whenever they wish. Furthermore, the Immigration and Naturalization Services would consider them long since to have been "grandfathered in" as American citizens.

---

[1] Known to Natives as "The Other Canal Street", the Canal Street in the Shambles is often confused by tourists and the uninitiated with the much longer and more impressive Canal Street upon which Union Station and the original Maxwell Street Market can be found. While there have been a number of attempts to change the name of "The Other Canal Street" to East Canal Street, North Canal Street, Little Venice, or the Loop, the Shambles Residents Association has protested any change of name, often violently, as the confusion of names has often been a source of amusement, revenue, or food to the locals. Many of the people who eat once at Molly Graw's are lost, some of them for good.

A Walking Tour of The Shambles

Do not, however, out of consideration for local customs, mention this to the Swandoliers. Any mention of the I.N.S. makes them uncomfortable, and they are likely accidentally to knock you overboard in their agitation.)

This is the true explanation for the Rialto-style stone footbridge that crosses Canal Street midway. Any other explanations you may hear, in Gavagan's Saloon or in Molly Graw's Restaurant, are "leg-pulls" by Shambles locals with a fine sense of humour.

If you have begun your tour of the Shambles early, you will find **Molly Graw's Restaurant** the ideal spot for a late lunch — or a quite normal one, if you have skipped the Petting Zoo. If you began your walking tour in the afternoon, Molly Graw's is just the place for dinner. And should you return next morning for that must-have item you passed over in the Shambles Shop (where else are your going to find wax Ugly Fruit?), why not try Molly Graw's for breakfast? We may think its blend of Chicago, Southern, and British cuisines odd, and in fact we do. But be prepared to let out your belt.

"Wisdom is nearer when we soup than when we sear," reads the inscription over Molly's door and it fits her cozy restaurant to a T. It is unpretentious (although reservations are taken for dinner and from Native Americans). It is homey to a fault — our waitress positively compelled us to finish our turnip greens with smoking pigs' trotters before she would consent to serve our green tomato pie and watermelon a la mode. And it has a rollicking sense of humor. When we mentioned that the service seemed slow, another waitress explained, quite deadpan, that most of the servers were dead. As we left, we noticed our own waitress wearing our tip upon her eyes. She had crazy glue and mortuary wax, our informant told us, in her makeup kit.

We leave Molly Graw's by the rear exit, which deposits us beside **Hair Today** (listed in old guidebooks as *Sawney's Barbershop*, and still under its original management). Do we need a shave? A haircut? A good old-fashioned restorative bleeding? Their prices are reasonable, and the hairdressers are delightful, friendly and amusing. "Hair today," they chuckle, as they lead you to the chair in the centre of the room, "and gone tomorrow!"

They maintain the traditions of the profession, including the free haircut for locals upon their birthdays. They are also extremely proud of the fact that they raise their own leeches; according to the barber who shaved one of your authors on his birthday, several years ago, the only commercially viable leech farm in the Chicago area is located in the basement of this establishment. Alas, a prior engagement forced us to decline the offer to inspect it closer.

Go left.

In all probability you will come out on Canal Street. If this does not happen, you should close your eyes and retrace your steps, and pray. Or perhaps you could take note of where you are, of its stores and landmarks, its street names and any sites of historical interest. *The Little Walks For Sightseers* series always needs contributors, should you manage to find your way home. Such things have been known.

Cross Canal street.

Neil Gaiman and Gene Wolfe

The apartment buildings you are looking at were built in 1910 by Horsten Vorm, a successful horse-feed merchant, who had come to America as a boy from Thule, and who wished to set up a place where Thulian immigrants could be comfortable among their own kind, at room prices only marginally higher than they would have to pay to live among the "sklipsey bool" as those not from Thule were known. Horsten Vorm was applauded in his day for never turning a single person from his native land away from his door.

The words above the door "Florlach Drelma Sklipsey Kras Bool Nornyar" is a pun in Thulian: it means both "Cheap rooms available here, no infidels permitted" and also "Cheap horse-feed makes us all rich. Ask inside for details."

Note the pipes on the outer wall. These were used on Sunday by the orthodox, older Thulians, to dispose of the neat's-foot oil that accumulated during the week. Now they are purely ornamental.

Today the apartment building is inhabited by people of all races and beliefs. Still, as recently as 1978, builders performing renovations reported problems with elderly Thulians being discovered in crawlspaces, ventilation ducts, and in boarded-up stairwells, all of them with up-to-date rent-books and current leases. It is not known who they were paying rent to, although the rent was certainly being collected.

A Walking Tour of The Shambles

Note the carving of the twisted face on the iron drainpipe cover.

Once you have done this, check your wallet. Place it in an inner pocket, or better still, remove ten dollars from it, then place your wallet in an envelope and mail it to yourself from the mailbox on the corner. Put the ten dollar bill in your right shoe. This is the recommended course of action for anyone entering Gavagan's Irish Saloon.

There are many, many interesting things to see at **Gavagan's Irish Saloon**, many interesting people to talk to, and their bar is without parallel in the Chicago area. It is unfortunate that neither of your authors has yet made it out of Gavagan's without a badly beer-soaked notebook, or with much in the way of hard facts. When was it built? Who owns it? Is there any person named Gavagan in anyway involved with the bar or its operations? What is the significance of the severed finger in the bottle of Pudsey's Mild Pale Ale that hangs from a length of barbed wire above the bar? We do not know, nor do we believe that the regulars know either, no matter what they may say. They are coarse, fanciful people, and easily amused.

Nota Bene: Visitors to Gavagan's should pay close attention to the notice attached to the wall beside the front door, in small print. For those with poor eyesight, or who feel uncomfortable standing for too long outside Gavagan's, we take this opportunity to reproduce it here (with permission).

> *The Chicago Police department requires us to remind sightseers that the following activities are illegal within Chicago City Limits: Bear-baiting; bull baiting; salmon-baiting; soliciting minors for immoral purposes; theft; gopher baiting; interfering with the eggs or nests of bald eagles or other protected birds; organ-baiting; simony; premature burial; the pigeon drop; robbery with menaces; robbery without menaces but with a short iron bar; public drunkenness; driving a vehicle while intoxicated; disturbing the peace; eradicating stool-pigeons; dog baiting; soliciting sexual favors with menaces; uttering forged banknotes; spitting; rat-baiting without a license.*

Alas, it has been twenty years since a member of the Chicago Police Department has been seen in Gavagan's Irish Saloon, and we would hazard that the majority of the squeaks, squeals and howls that signal another enthusiastic rat-baiting in the back room are completely unlicensed.

Leaving Gavagan's Irish Saloon, and returning

A Walking Tour of The Shambles

to Canal Street, a visitor looks from side to side, hunting for landmarks or for anything familiar, wondering why it is now dark. "How long was I in there? How much did I drink? What has happened to my right shoe?" These are just a few of the questions sightseers might well ask themselves at this point in the walking tour.

(Further questions for sightseers will be found at the end of this booklet, along with a bibliography and some useful maps [omitted in this edition, on legal advice] and a selection of recipes from Molly Graw's.)

Walk north up Canal Street.

Hurry your pace. Step up. Look lively.

The wind is blowing cold, now.

The footsteps you hear are your own, in echo. Do they not start when you start, stop when you stop? The dragging noise is simply a property of the acoustics of the region.

Do not run. Do not show fear. Do not stop walking, whatever else you do.

Look around you, casually. Listen for a car; it might be a taxi, after all. You can dream. But do not stop walking. Keep on.

Beyond this point, there are no street lamps.

There. Now you have visited the Shambles. Have you seen all the sights? We doubt it. We have not begun to list the side-alleys, the enchanting byways, of the region. Also we have intentionally omitted several key landmarks.

Limitations of space alone, combined with editorial direction, have kept the Saunders Memorial Hospital, the Coven Garden Opera House, and the unique Whispering Gallery, out of this booklet. We commend to our readers the forthcoming *Little Walks For Sightseers Number 17*, in which these charming nooks, and many others, will be revealed.

The Shambles has been compared by visitors to an onion, to Venice, even to Walt Disney World: there is more there than a casual sightseer can ever hope to take in in one day. There is too much to experience, too much to see, too much to taste and touch for a day, or even a week.

Often, as the locals are only too pleased to tell you, it will take your life.

FIN

A Walking Tour of The Shambles

Further Questions

As you walk (or run, as many prefer), along Canal Street, a few questions concerning the Shambles and its unique history may remain. Below we list those that occurred to us after our own tour, and others that friends and acquaintances have put to us when apprised of our visit. In addition, we supply the best answers we have found. Some are admittedly tentative.

- **The first is sure to be, "At what point will I have left the Shambles?"**

If you are proceeding south on Canal, at 27th Street. If north, 35th. But in a larger and better sense, we who leave the Shambles never forsake it entirely. Nor does it forsake us. If you included your address when you signed the guest book in Cereal House, you may well learn the truth of this as soon as you get home. If not, it may take days.

- **"Do I have all my credit cards?"**

Unless you stayed at Cereal House, ate at Molly Graw's, or bought something in the Shambles Shop or the gift shop in the House of Clocks, the answer may well be yes. You did not allow the verger to persuade you to be make a donation, did you? And permit him to charge it to a credit card?

- **"Who was the young man seated on the shared grave of Paul Burns and Jenny Ashe, victims of the Chicago Fire?"**

Probably another tourist, unless his clothing appeared markedly out of date.

Neil Gaiman and Gene Wolfe

- **"Why isn't this district better known?"**

Well, we're doing all we can. Too many sightseers just lock themselves in their rooms and cry when friends and family inquire. A box on them!

- **"Why do I feel that I am being followed?"**

Quite possibly you are. "Horla" Kelly is prone to this. So is his cousin Ms. Link, the Girl Detective. Check the street behind you, not too obviously. You might feign to inspect your makeup in the mirror of your compact, for example, assuming that you are a woman or are lying in a box. Others may find it useful to return to scrutinize something in a shop window. Make three right turns in quick succession. (Be careful here; two right turns will return you to the Shambles.) Enter some public building and go into a restroom intended for the opposite sex. Exit quickly, if possible by another door.

- **"If there really are no catacombs beneath The First Church of the Sailor Return'd, why does everyone say there are? Whence came that clamor, as of cats in torment?"**

There really are no catacombs. The catacombs are in Rome. There is, however, an extensive network of underground galleries linking the Shambles with the Deep Tunnel Project, and so with the Underworld. Warning: HARD HAT AREA. The echoes there distort the human voice.

- **"What possible pleasure could anyone find in murdering women and dissolving their bodies in acid, and is there a place where that might be done safely today?"**

A Walking Tour of The Shambles

You are passing Number 13 Canal Street, walking in the wrong direction. Turn around. Keep repeating that you wish to go to the Loop. If possible, repeat it to a cab driver.

- **"What was the import of the poison pen letter received by Miss Flora Lovat in 1912?"**

You see, you should have purchased the facsimile of that letter in the gift shop of the House of Clocks. Or at least read one while pretending you might buy a copy if the contents pleased you. The letter made three principal points: First, that its author was Harold Brennan, that he was still alive and residing in an empty resort hotel on the Michigan shore of Lake Michigan, and that he wished to wed Miss Lovat. Second, that they were already married, and that he would return to her as soon as he recalled their home address. And third, that she as a loyal wife and paramour was to retrieve his body from the graveyard behind the prison and see it decently interred in the churchyard of The First Church of the Sailor Return'd, and sacrifice there upon her next visit to Chicago. It also alleged that Strephon was her illegitimate son, and warned her against fulfilling a future commitment at Coven Garden Theater. (Later the site of her death.)

FAVORITE DISHES & RECIPES FROM
MOLLY GRAW'S RESTAURANT

Breakfast. Try the hot broiled grapefruit with kippers. Or grilled grapefruit with Ginger. (Ginger will gladly sit at your side, share your food, and talk to you.) Cheese grits with red-eye gravy makes an excellent side dish; Molly's red-eyes are unexcelled. finish up with a Krispy Kreme Do-nut. Or several. Don't forget the chicory coffee, a real New Orleans treat. (You can improve this further with a discreet shot of bourbon, Southern Comfort, or both.)

Alternative Breakfasts: Brain and eggs, fried green tomatoes, and beaten biscuits with persimmon butter. (You will actually hear your biscuits screaming in the kitchen, a rare treat.) Or chicken-and hash, sweet 'tater biscuits, scrapple with sorghum, and scones with curdled cream. For the Chicago minded: a frosty mug of Old Chicago Beer. Your waitress will gladly break a fertile egg into it upon request. Stir, drink, and run for mayor! For something more substantial, eight eggs with gunpowder butter served over Polish Potato Pancakes, with a double shot of real bootleg hooch. A favorite of Big Al's.

Here is a breakfast dish that really struck our fancy. (Used without permission.) Knock-Down Kedgeree: 4 oz. brown rice, a pound or more of smoked smelt, water, milk, hard-boiled eggs, one half cup parsley, one half cup butter, one quarter cup Bombay Curry Powder, two tablespoons cayenne pepper. Cook the rice and poach the smelt (or shad, if smelt is not available) in the water and milk. Save some parsley and an egg. Mix everything else together, stirring hard. Sprinkle the saved parsley and egg on top. Warm in hot oven, serve piping hot with plenty of free ice water.

Lunch. On a hot day, try Molly's cold broiled tongue (no need to worry, she will get another) with the dandelion-and-roadkill salad, lemon ice and a Scarlet O'Hara. Wow! In colder weather, smothered rabbit, hot mush, and shoo-fly pie. Porter to drink. (Stir until porter dissolves completely.) For the true taste of Chicago, deep-dish stuffed pizza with Molly's famous long-pig Italian sausage and head cheese. For a little taste of an Old English Garden, toad-in whole, made with genuine, authentic ingredients. For a somewhat larger taste of the Old English Grocery, order the Trout in Milk. Or bubble-and-shriek. True gourmets will surely appreciate the Liver Pâté en Kraût.

Another favorite recipe, (used without permission). Arctic Horseradish: 1/2 barrel whipping cream, one large or two small horses grated, ten to twenty radishes grated, barrel wine vinegar (or other vinegars, or lemon juice), salt to taste, box ground pepper. Whip cream. Mix and freeze for a cold weather dessert. A nice change from ice cream. This recipe is said to have finished several expeditions.

Tea. As well as such standard black teas as Orange Pekoe, Oolong, and Georgia Brown, more than a hundred Herb teas are a available. Included are nightshade, spider-lily, dog rose, rose hip, dog hip, diatom (an excellent choice for those seeking to gain weight), channel wrack, kaffir corn, pop corn, ergot (high tea only), shoo fly agaric, and mock-orange and hop. Most are from Herb's own garden. Your choice of sandwiches will vary day by day; but baked apple, dried fruit medley, sardine paste, minced mussel, and catfish-and-kimchi on raisin bread are perennial favorites served almost every day. With the sandwiches, ever so many sweet treats—apple slices spread with apple butter, Oreos dusted with Ovaltine powder, Moon Pies, Walnettos, Brown Sugar Bears, fudge (chocolate, double chocolate, and Mississippi Mud), Snickerdoodles, pistachio shells stuffed with Peanut Butter, Deviled Ham cookies, scones with lemon curdle and/or Dee-von cream, Valomilks, chocolate dipped Jelly Sticks, Wilbur Buds, Goo Goos, Whorehound Drops Sally Lunn, Cherry Mash Trash, milkweed nonpareils, fruit-free fruit shoes, Walnettos, Black Walnettos, Chocolate Bitter Almond Toffee (made right in Molly Graw's kitchen since 1963), Bing-bang bars, "rabbit bones" (a crunchy Easter delight), Liquorice Somesorts, Scent-Scents. And much more. We could not get over Molly's Real Old-fashioned Coconut Rainbow Candy — after two pieces we stood on our chair and demanded that somebody surrender Dorothy. Molly's Necko Wafers are made with real neck, something we never expected to see again. You can suck on an old-fashioned liquorice gas pipe, or feast guiltily upon chocolate or vanilla babies. (But watch out for the bones.) Walnettos.

FAVORITES FROM MOLLY GRAW'S RESTAURANT

Dinner. No question about it, you should start with the shinbone soup. After that Saunders Squash with Catfish Stuffing. (Radish pudding is the only dessert.) Or Beachcombers Gumbo with sizzling scalped oysters and blackbottom pie. How about Country Captain (market price), Sour Cider Salad, and Beet Duff (or savory Turnip Duff for dessert? try Galatine of Liver, with Liverpool University Sauce, a hearty dinner sure to stick to your ribs. For the more daring Curate of Mutton with Opium Sauce. For a light dinner after the theatre, Wood Coldcock. Molly's Beer Battered Violets go well with this.

Here's the recipe for one of Molly's dinner favorites, and too favorite desserts, two! Liver, Lights, and Larkspur Stew (used without permission): 1 pound hog tripe, 1 pound hog liver, 1 pound hog jowl shaved, 1 pound hog brains, 1/2 pound lard, 1 skunk egg, salt, pepper, chili pepper. Kill the hog first. Cut up everything and mix it good. Cover with boiling water. Simmer on low heat overnight. Thicken with flowers and serve. Tastes as good as it smells.

Desserts: Cracker Pie (used without permission): 1 Georgia Cracker, 300 egg whites, 1 barrel sugar, 1/4 keg baking soda, 20 chopped dates (these need not be old dates of the Cracker's; anybody's dates will do), lots of nuts. Break up the Cracker. Beat egg whites and dates until stiff. Bone. Mix in the rest. Cook in greased pans, moderate oven, 20 minutes or less. Good hot or cold, with Dreem Whip or ice cream. Or plain.

Bonus recipe (used without persimmon). Poor Folks Pudding; 1 cup sugar, 1 cup milk, as much vanilla as sister left in the bottle, salt, egg, melted butter if you got any, some flour. Cat or small dog named Fluffy. Whip the egg. Add some sugar and beat Fluffy. Fold in all the rest, alternating. Bake until done. Serve with, Pump Water Sauce: 2 cups boiled water, lots of sugar, butter, salt, cornponestarch (dissolved like the porter, but smaller), nutmeg. Bust up the nutmeg if you cannot grate it. Mix everything together and simmer on the stove while the pudding is busy inside. Pour hot over pudding and serve.

A Walking Tour of The Shambles

Further Reading

"And Never Call Me Captain": The Lives and Time of John Saunders
E. R. Postlethwaite (Horrig and Banter, 1981)

An indispensable biography of the man Theodore Roosevelt described as "an American to the marrow-bone". Several contemporary photographs and oil paintings help bring Saunders to life. Unfortunately this book contains only a paragraph (on page 243) about the Shambles, claiming erroneously that the man known in Chicago as "Captain" John Saunders was in fact another man of the same name.

H.H. Holmes: The Monster of Old Street
Gervase Brinkman (Orig. 1921, reprinted SplatteryWine Press, 1995)

The House of Seven Horrors
Lorna Filmore (Knopf, 1933)

"—a gallstone, a glass eye, a gold tooth and a nightmare—" Meditations on H.H. Holmes's House of Horrors.
Flitch, Barkwell, Snipes, et al. (The Vanity Press, 1950)

My Life as a Snoop
Daniel Murphy (Enterprising Press, 1901)

A small sampling of the books about H. H. Holmes and his house. Fashion in monsters sweeps Holmes into and out of the spotlight, decade by decade. The poems in the *Meditations* are remarkable for the view that they give into how Holmes was perceived in the aftermath of World War II, and for the essay by Amanda Flitch on the origins of the common childrens' song that begins "There was a little feller, and they found him in the cellar, and his skin was going yeller and his eyes had

A Walking Tour of The Shambles

gone away . . ." and links it conclusively with the *Police Gazette* description of the initial walk through the Holmes House on Hallowe'en of 1884.

> *One Wacky Woman: Margaux Brown and Her Wonderful World!*
> Jim Allen (House of Clocks Press, 1955, revised and reissued 1970)

An oddly unsatisfying read. The photographs of Miss Brown and her clocks are initially exciting, then charming, but ultimately depressing. The guide to the House of Clocks is long on puns, short on facts. (A sample: "In the alcove is the Koschei Speaking Clock — but watch out! It may want you to sit down and listen for an HOUR to its CLOCK-TALES! Yup — for this little fella it's always CLOCK-TALE HOUR!!")

> *In Meat We Trust: An Authorised and True History of the International Brotherhood of Meatworkers.*
> Various Authors (IBMw Press, 1973)

> *We Are The Dead: Confessions From Former Members of The International Brotherhood of Meatworkers*
> Anonymous (Horrig and Banter, 1997)

Our stomachs were not strong enough to finish *We Are The Dead*, and we are men who have eaten at Molly Graw's. If you can find it, or finish it, you are a better man than either of us. But then, you knew that.

> *Molly Graw's Greatest Recipes*
> The Staff of Molly Graw's Restaurant (Workman, 1981)

> *Molly Graw's Greatest Party Recipes*
> The Staff of Molly Graw's Restaurant (Workman, 1984)

Neil Gaiman and Gene Wolfe

Molly Graw's 1001 Disturbing Things to do with Leftovers
The Staff of Molly Graw's Restaurant (Workman, 1990)

Botulism, Salmonella or E-Coli? Common Bacteria Easily Identified
The Staff of Molly Graw's Restaurant (Horrig and Banter, 1996)

We are indebted to Molly and her staff for committing their recipes to paper; and feel that we should point out that anyone who uses even one of these recipes in her own kitchen should be similarly committed.

A Hundred Charming Architectural Oddities In the Chicago Area
Lamont Pickle (Rot Press, 1936)

It is astonishing how little time has touched the Shambles. While the greater part of the other architectural oddities and marvels listed in this fine book have succumbed to the ravages of time and progress, the Shambles has remained untouched. (The farrago of speculations on why this might be in Chapter Seven of *We Are The Dead* are an obvious attempt to blacken the name of a fine organisation, which has done so much for local charities and for the neighbourhood.)

Ghost Stories of Old Street Illustrated
Chromosome Foxness. Illustrated by Diverse Hands. (Shambles Press, updated annually)

As ultimately invaluable as it is unreliable, much like the work you are holding. Thus, we part, with one admonishment: *Caveat Lector,* always and forever.

ALSO AVAILABLE FROM
AMERICAN FANTASY™

INVISIBLE PLEASURES
by Mary Frances Zambreno

"Her strong women transcend the times in which they live, whether it's the difficult past—or even the more difficult future. So once again, I say: 'Write more, damn it!' Please."
—Jane Yolen, author of *The Devil's Arithmetic*

"Undiscovered gems of genre fiction are not so rare after all, and they're a lot easier to deal with for me when they come packed together in a nice collection like this."
— Rick Kleffel, The Agony Column

"Well, this is an excellent collection by one of the best writers of fantasy that I have ever encountered. . . . I highly recommend it."
—Sam Tomaino, SF Revu.com

"Zambreno writes psychologically astute historical fiction, as well as sensitive fantasy, but don't underestimate her twisted sense of humor. Those looking for an anthology of unusual and varied subjects should read *Invisible Pleasures* for its own merits . . . and not just because Jane Yolen said so."
— Elizabeth Allen, Tangent Online

"*Invisible Pleasures* is sure to please dedicated science fiction and fantasy fans who will appreciate her individualistic style and storytelling ability. Very highly recommended. . . . *Invisible Pleasures* is the perfect introduction to the talented Mary Frances Zambreno." —Midwest Book Review

American Fantasy is proud to present *Invisible Pleasures,* the critically-acclaimed short story collection by Mary Frances Zambreno, author of *A Plague of Sorcerers* and *Journeyman Wizard*. In this beautiful hardcover, you'll discover over a dozen intriguing stories of fantasy, sf, horror and mystery, including the popular "The Way Out," "Miss Emily's Roses" and "The Ghost in the Summer Kitchen."

Cover Art by Spectrum Artist Douglas Klauba.

$25.00 plus $5.00 Shipping/Handling
Order Online with Paypal at: **www.americanfantasypress.com**
Or send a check or money order to
American Fantasy, 919 Tappan St., Woodstock, IL, 60098

HUMOR

Gene Wolfe and Neil Gaiman invite you to tour the Shambles, that historic old Chicago neighborhood which miraculously survived the Great Fire of 1871. ("Ya can't burn Hell," as one local politician laughingly remarked.) Uniquely Chicago, the Shambles offers an array of delights for the intrepid sightseer: Cereal House with its Terribly Strange Bed (be sure to fill out the "next of kin" form if you stay the night: a quaint touch adding to the fun of an overnight visit); the House of Clocks boasts a collection of 20,000 time pieces — make sure you arrive on the hour, for an unforgettable moment; the historic H.H. Holmes' House with the bars on his children's windows still intact; Saunders Park, a soothing respite from the city streets (if one is careful), with its gardens, statuary, ornamental lake and the infamous Petting Zoo (a favorite with children, but it's best not to bring your own); plus many more intriguing sights . . .

In the finest tradition of Charles Addams and Edward Gorey, our trustworthy guides Neil Gaiman and Gene Wolfe reveal the secrets of the Shambles, finding the best places to eat, (and where *not* to accept food under any circumstances), where to begin your walking tour, and when to run.

The Shambles has been called a place of dark magic and deadly menace. Many will insist there is no such place. Most *pray* it does not exist. Certainly, a spot not to be missed by any avid sightseer.

Come along . . . walk lively, now. The inhabitants of the Shambles are dying to meet you.

This lovely edition of *A Walking Tour of the Shambles* sports a cover by Gahan Wilson, America's reigning King of Whimsical Terrors, plus interior illustrations of Shambles' locales by Randy Broecker and Earl Geier, two daring Chicagoans.

Cover by Gahan Wilson

American Fantasy Press
919 Tappan Street
Woodstock, Illinois 60098
americanfantasypress.com

$15.00

ISBN-13: 978-096103526-6
ISBN-10:   096103526-9

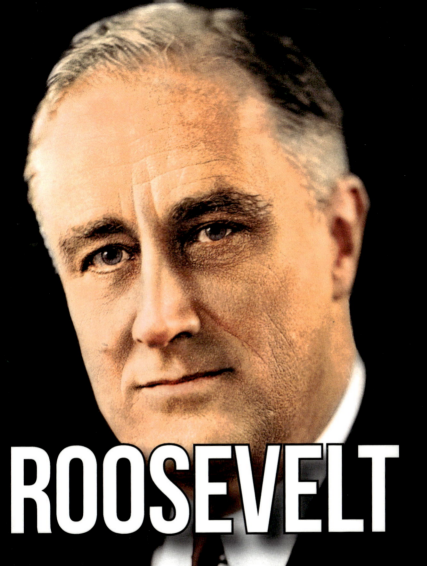

ROOSEVELT

NOTHING TO FEAR

ALEXANDER KENNEDY